Hello Kitty's
Lucky Day!

By Kris Hirschmann
Illustrated by Sachiho Hino

SCHOLASTIC INC.

New York   Toronto   London   Auckland   Sydney
Mexico City   New Delhi   Hong Kong   Buenos Aires

Decorate all of the
pictures in this book with
stickers. The page numbers
on the sticker page will
help you figure out which
stickers to use.

ISBN-13: 978-0-439-87134-1
ISBN-10: 0-439-87134-4

12 11 10 9 8 7 6 5 4 3 2 1   7 8 9 10 11 12/0

Designed by Angela Jun and Amy Heinrich
Printed in the U.S.A.
First printing, March 2007

Contents

Chapter 1
Luck of the Irish

Hello Kitty walked into her classroom one spring morning. Right away she saw a green card sitting on her desk. The card was cut in the shape of a clover.

Hello Kitty looked around the classroom. Green clover cards sat on every desk.

"What are these clovers, Mr. Bearly?" she asked the teacher.

"They are called shamrocks,

Hello Kitty. I made them because tomorrow is St. Patrick's Day," Mr. Bearly said as the rest of the students came into the room. "It is a day to remember Irish traditions and symbols. And shamrocks are very Irish!"

Jody raised his hand as he sat down. "What are some other Irish things?" he asked.

"Well, in one Irish story, little elves called leprechauns hide pots of gold," said Mr. Bearly. "If you find the end of a rainbow, you'll find the gold."

"Ooooh!" said everyone.

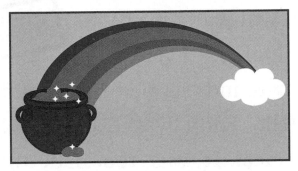

"Wearing green is one way to celebrate St. Patrick's Day," Mr. Bearly continued. "Most important of all, though, is the idea of good LUCK. And that brings me back to the shamrocks. Tomorrow, one of you is going to get very lucky. Write a name on your shamrock card. Then put the card into this box." Mr. Bearly touched a box on his desk. "We will pull out one card. The person whose name is on it will win a pizza."

"Hooray!" Everyone shouted and clapped their hands.

Hello Kitty was excited. What a fun idea! It was too bad, though, that there could only be one winner. *I wish everyone could be* lucky, she thought.

Suddenly Hello Kitty had an idea. "Maybe I could *make* my friends lucky," she said to herself. "Everyone would be so happy—and making friends happy is a great way to celebrate *any* holiday!"

The more Hello Kitty thought about it, the better she liked her idea.

"I'm sure I can do it," she said. "With just a little luck, it will be the best St. Patrick's Day ever!"

St. Patrick's Day Symbols:

- Leprechauns
- Rainbows
- Pots of gold
- Shamrocks

Wear GREEN to celebrate!

How Lucky!

Some shamrocks have four leaves. These shamrocks, called four-leaf clovers, are extra lucky!

Chapter 2
Big Plans

At home that night, Hello Kitty prepared for her big day. She thought she knew how to make her schoolmates lucky, but it was going to take some work.

Hello Kitty sat at her craft table. She pulled out some green paper. She drew three hearts and a rectangle on the paper. She used scissors to cut out the shapes. Then she glued them together to make a shamrock.

Next Hello Kitty got out a marker. She used the marker to write on the shamrock.

When Hello Kitty was done, she held the shamrock up and looked at it. "How cute!" she said. She put the shamrock aside, then got right to work making more. Soon there was a big stack of green shamrocks on the table.

Hello Kitty smiled as she slipped

the stack into her backpack. "Everyone will love these," she said to herself. Just thinking about it made her feel happy and excited.

To make shamrocks just like the ones Hello Kitty made, follow the instructions on page 48.

Hello Kitty was even more excited about the surprise she had planned for her sister, Mimmy, the next morning. She could hardly wait for St. Patrick's Day to arrive!

How Lucky!

Some people think the numbers 3 and 7 are lucky. What's your lucky number?

Chapter 3
Mimmy's Green Bow

Hello Kitty woke up very early. "Hooray! St. Patrick's Day is here!" she cried. It was time to put her first plan into action.

Hello Kitty got out of bed. She crept down the hallway, trying not to make any noise. She opened the door to Mimmy's room and peeked inside. Mimmy was still fast asleep.

Hello Kitty entered the room and tiptoed over to Mimmy's dresser.

As quietly as she could, she opened the drawer where Mimmy kept her bows. She put a big green bow  right on top of the pile. Then she slid the drawer shut.

Just then Hello Kitty heard a big yawn from the bed. Mimmy was awake!

"Good morning, Hello Kitty," Mimmy said sleepily. She yawned again and rubbed her eyes. "What are you doing in my room?"

"I . . . um . . . I lost my favorite bow," Hello Kitty stammered. "I thought you might have it."

"I'll look for you," said Mimmy. She got out of bed, walked to her dresser, and opened the drawer. Right away she spotted the new green bow.

"Oh, how pretty!" Mimmy cried. "This must be a St. Patrick's Day surprise from Mama. I love it! It's lucky it was right on top—I might have forgotten to wear something green today."

Mimmy picked up the bow and put it on. She was

so happy that she forgot all about Hello Kitty's lost bow.

Hello Kitty was happy, too. Her plan had worked! She smiled at her sister. "That *is* lucky, Mimmy," she said. "Now I'd better go and put on

something green, too. It's almost time to leave for school—and I have a feeling it's going to be a great day!"

Dear Diary,

Mimmy doesn't have a green bow. I think I'll put a brand-new one into her drawer while she sleeps. I'll have to be very quiet so I don't wake her up.

How Lucky!

If you find a penny, you'll have good luck all day long—but only if the penny is heads-up.

Chapter 4
A Lucky Find

Hello Kitty and Mimmy got to school before the first bell rang. Mimmy ran straight to the playground to show everyone her new bow.

Hello Kitty went in the other direction. When she was sure no one could see her, she took the lucky shamrocks out of her backpack and hid them everywhere she could think of.

When all the ſhamrockſ were gone, Hello Kitty walked to the playground. "Happy St. Patrick's Day, everyone!" she said when she got there.

"Happy St. Patrick's Day to you, too!" replied her friends.

Just then the bell rang. All of the friends headed for the school building. Hello Kitty whispered to Jody, "Let's go a different way. We can race everybody to the classroom."

"That sounds like fun!" said Jody.

Hello Kitty ran off with Jody following her. She led her friend right to a place where she had dropped a lucky shamrock. She wanted to make sure Jody would see the surprise she had left.

It worked! Jody suddenly stopped running. "What's this?" he said. He reached down and picked up the shamrock. "This says I'll have good luck all day long," he said.

Jody grinned. "I'm glad we came this way," he said.

"And I'm glad because you're glad," said Hello Kitty. "That makes me lucky, too. I guess it's just that kind of day!"

Chapter 5
Sweet Surprise

Jody and Hello Kitty started walking toward the classroom again. A moment later, something caught Hello Kitty's eye. A brightly colored sign was taped to the wall.

"Go on without me, Jody," said Hello Kitty. "I'll catch up."

After Jody left, Hello Kitty read the sign.

"Hmmmm," said Hello Kitty as she walked away.

"That gives me an idea."

In the classroom, the morning flew by. Soon it was time for recess. When the bell rang, Hello Kitty went over to Kathy's desk.

"Do you want to go to the Sweet Shoppe, Kathy?" she asked. She didn't say anything about the sign she had seen.

"I would love to," said Kathy. "Let's go!"

Before long, the friends were standing outside the Sweet Shoppe. Kathy pushed open the door.

"Happy St. Patrick's Day!" shouted the storekeeper as soon as Kathy and Hello Kitty stepped into the store. "Come and get your free treat!" He handed each friend a chocolate coin wrapped in gold foil.

"Thank you! What a nice surprise!" said Kathy as she unwrapped the candy. She popped the sweet

coin into her mouth. "I just love chocolate. It's lucky we came here today, Hello Kitty."

"Yes, it is," Hello Kitty said with a smile. Her idea had worked out perfectly. "This day just keeps getting better and better!"

Dear Diary,

I bet I can find extra ways to make my friends "lucky." I'll just keep my eyes open and pay attention to little things.

How Lucky!

Some people carry a rabbit's foot for good luck.

Chapter 6
Colors of the Rainbow

After recess, it was time for art class. On the way to class, Hello Kitty heard something interesting. "I won a prize! I knew the colors of the rainbow in order," someone from an earlier class was saying.

Maybe the teacher has a prize for us, too, thought Hello Kitty. There was enough time to visit the school library. She would do some reading before class, just in case.

Sure enough, when art class started, the teacher handed out paper, paints, and brushes. "I want you to paint rainbows in honor of St. Patrick's Day . . . and there may be a surprise later," she said.

Everyone started to work. Soon the classroom was buzzing with activity.

"Do you know how to remember the colors of the rainbow?" Hello Kitty said quietly to her friend Thomas.  "You say ROY G. BIV. That stands for Red, Orange, Yellow, Green, Blue, Indigo, Violet."

"Neat!" said Thomas. "I'm going to paint my rainbow just like that."

"Not me," said Hello Kitty. "I'm making mine all green for St. Patrick's Day."

Soon everyone was finished. The teacher walked around the room, looking at all the pretty rainbows. When she reached Thomas's desk, she stopped and picked up Thomas's painting.

"These colors are in exactly the

right order," she said.
"Good job, Thomas. You get a sticker." Thomas blushed with pride as the teacher put the sticker on his shirt.

"It's so lucky you told me about the rainbow, Hello Kitty!" Thomas said as everyone left the classroom. "Winning that sticker made me feel good. It's too bad you didn't paint your rainbow the same way."

"I don't mind," said Hello Kitty. "I like my green rainbow—and I liked seeing you get the sticker." She gave Thomas a big hug. "Now come on. It's time for lunch. I bet we're having something green. It *is* St. Patrick's Day, after all!"

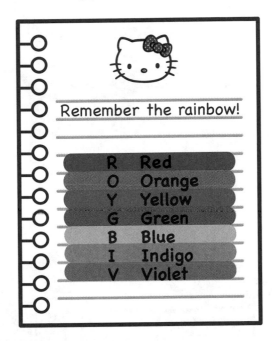

Remember the rainbow!

R	Red
O	Orange
Y	Yellow
G	Green
B	Blue
I	Indigo
V	Violet

How Lucky!

It is considered lucky to see three butterflies at the same time.

Chapter 7
The Truth Comes Out

In the lunchroom, Mimmy, Jody, Kathy, and Thomas sat together at a table. They were saving a seat for Hello Kitty, who was still filling her tray.

"Look what I found," said Jody. He pulled out his lucky shamrock.

"Oh! I heard about these," said Mimmy. "Everyone is finding them.

I wonder who made them?"

"Someone nice," said Kathy.

"Someone who likes making people happy," said Thomas.

"Hello Kitty!" they all said together.

"You know what?" Mimmy said slowly. "I think Hello Kitty has been very busy today! I found her in my room this morning. I bet she left this green bow for me."

"She was with me when I found my shamrock," said Jody. "She led me right to it."

"I got a free chocolate coin—and

it was Hello Kitty's idea to visit the candy store," said Kathy.

"And Hello Kitty told me about the rainbow colors," said Thomas. "That's the only reason I got this sticker. It all makes perfect sense."

The friends sat quietly for a moment. They thought about what a good friend Hello Kitty was.

Finally Jody spoke. "Hello Kitty has worked so hard to make us feel lucky, I wish we could do something special for her," he said.

"Maybe we can," said Kathy. "I have an idea!"

Kathy told everyone her plan. All the friends agreed it was a great idea.

Just then Hello Kitty arrived with her lunch tray. "Is everyone having a good St. Patrick's Day?" she asked as she sat down.

"Oh, yes," everyone answered. The friends grinned at one another. Hello Kitty didn't know it yet, but it was her turn to be lucky!

Lunch Menu:

Spinach pie
Green beans
Sweet peas
Lime sherbet

milk

How Lucky!

Sailors sometimes keep cats
on ships for good luck.

Chapter 8
Lucky Day

In class that afternoon, the friends learned all about St. Patrick's Day. Everyone had fun finding out about Ireland and Irish traditions.

Just before the end of the day, Mr. Bearly stood up. "It's time for our drawing," he said. "Hello Kitty, will you help me?"

"Of course," said Hello Kitty.

She walked to the front of the classroom. She lifted the lid off the

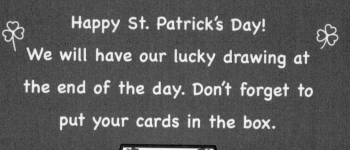

Happy St. Patrick's Day!
We will have our lucky drawing at
the end of the day. Don't forget to
put your cards in the box.

box and pulled out a card—with her name on it. "I won! It's my lucky day!" she shouted. She was so excited that she started jumping up and down.

But Hello Kitty jumped a little bit too hard. Her elbow flew out and bumped the box. The box tipped over, dumping green cards everywhere.

"Oh, no! I'm sorry!" gasped Hello

Kitty. She kneeled down to pick up the cards—and then she saw something very strange. Her name was written on every single card.

Suddenly Hello Kitty realized that everyone in the classroom was giggling. Even Mr. Bearly was smiling.

"What's going on?" said Hello Kitty.

"We put your name on our cards, Hello Kitty," said Kathy. "We found out about the things you did to make us feel lucky. We wanted to make you feel lucky, too."

"That is so sweet!" said Hello Kitty. "I do feel lucky, but not because of the drawing. I'm lucky because I have the best friends ever."

"And now you have a pizza, too!" said Jody.

Hello Kitty laughed. "You're  right, Jody. I do have a pizza. And a pizza is no fun to eat without friends to share it with," she said.

"Hooray!" cheered the class. "Thank you, Hello Kitty!"

"No. Thank *you*," said Hello Kitty. She smiled at everyone. "You taught me something important today. Good luck makes you happy for a moment, but good friends make you happy forever. I have the most wonderful friends anyone could hope for—and that makes me the luckiest girl in the world!"

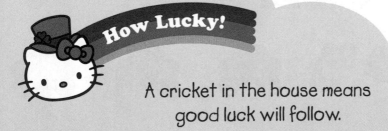

How Lucky!

A cricket in the house means good luck will follow.

Hello Kitty's Lucky Shamrocks

You can make lucky shamrocks, just like the ones Hello Kitty made!

1. Trace three hearts and one rectangle onto green paper. With adult supervision, cut out the shapes.

2. Spread glue on the edge of one heart. Put another heart on top. Press to stick the hearts together.

3. Spread glue on the edge of the third heart. Put the glued hearts on top. Press to stick everything together.

4. Spread glue on the top of the rectangle. Put the glued hearts on top. Press to stick everything together.

5. Use a marker to write a St. Patrick's Day message on the shamrock.

6. Decorate the shamrock any way you like. Give it to a friend or leave it lying around for someone to find.

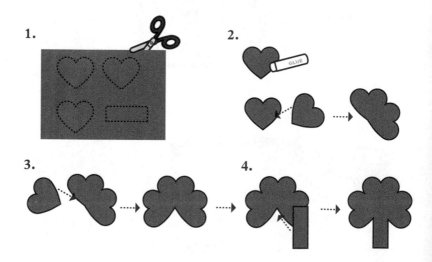

48